Welcome to Israel

By Elma Schemenauer

Published by The Child's World®
1980 Lookout Drive
Mankato, MN 56003-1705
800-599-READ
www.childsworld.com

Content Adviser: Professor Paul Sprachman, Vice Director,
Center for Middle Eastern Studies, Rutgers, The State University
of New Jersey, New Brunswick, NJ
Design and Production: The Creative Spark, San Juan Capistrano, CA
Editorial: Emily J. Dolbear, Brookline, MA
Photo Research: Deborah Goodsite, Califon, NJ

Cover image: A young Israeli in the city of Dimona in the Negev

Cover and title page: Jeremy Ferguson/Spectrum Photofile
Interior photos: Alamy: 8 (Hanan Isachar/Israel images), 3, 9 (Jean-Claude Carton/Bruce
Coleman Inc.), 3, 16 (Eddie Gerald); AP Photo: 29; The Art Archive: 10 (Archaeological
Museum Spalato/Dagli Orti (A)); Corbis: 15 (Ricki Rosen/SABA), 17 (David Rubinger),
22 (Envision); Getty Images: 7 (Chuck Fishman/The Image Bank), 12 (Uriel Sinai), 13
(Menahem Kahana/AFP), 20 (David Silverman), 21 (Ofira Yohanan/AFP); Israel Images:
25 (Karen Benzian), 27 (Richard Nowitz); iStockphoto.com: 11 (Deejpilot), 18 (Terry J.
Alcorn), 28 (Ufuk Zivana); Landov: 3, 19 (Debbie Hill/UPI), 30 (Ronen Zvulun/Reuters);
Lonely Planet Images: 31 (Oliver Strewe); NASA Earth Observatory: 4 (Reto Stockli);
Oxford Scientific: 6 (JTB Photo Communications Inc), 24 (Steve Vidler/Imagestate Ltd);
Panos Pictures: 23 (Philippe Lissac); SuperStock, Inc.: 14.
Map: XNR Productions: 5

Library of Congress Cataloging-in-Publication Data
Schemenauer, Elma.
  Welcome to Israel / Elma Schemenauer.
     p. cm. — (Welcome to the world)
  Includes index.
  ISBN-13: 978-1-59296-917-3 (library bound : alk. paper)
  ISBN-10: 1-59296-917-8 (library bound : alk. paper)
  1. Israel—Juvenile literature. I. Title.

DS126.5.S2843 2007
956.94—dc22
                    2007005558

Contents

Where Is Israel? 4

The Land 6

Plants and Animals 8

Long Ago 10

Israel Today 12

The People 14

City Life and Country Life 17

Schools and Language 18

Work 21

Food 22

Pastimes 24

Holidays 26

Fast Facts About Israel 28

How Do You Say... 30

Glossary 31

Further Information 32

Index 32

Where Is Israel?

Imagine you are on a spacecraft looking down at the planet Earth. You would see huge land areas with water around them. These land areas are called continents. Some continents are made up of several different countries. Israel is a small country on the continent of Asia. Israel's borders have often changed because Israel and the other countries in the region want control of certain areas.

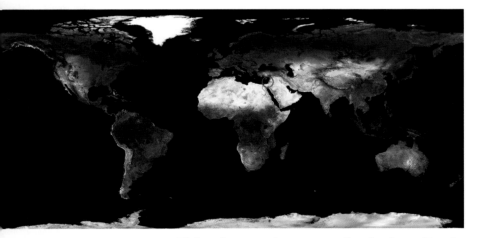

This picture gives us a flat look at Earth. Israel is inside the red circle.

4

ISRAEL

- ★ National capital
- • Other city
- - - - Disputed border

LEBANON

SYRIA

Golan
Heights

Nahariyya

Sea of
Galilee

Haifa

Nazareth

Mediterranean
Sea

Hadera

Netanya

Tel Aviv-Yafo · Petah Tiqwa
Bat Yam ·
Rishon LeZiyyon ·

West
Bank

Ashdod ·

Jerusalem ★

Ashqelon ·

Gaza
Strip

Dead
Sea

SAUDI
ARABIA

Beersheba

JORDAN

Dimona ·

N

W ⊗ E

S

Negev
Desert

0   20   40 miles

0   20   40 kilometers

EGYPT

SAUDI
ARABIA

Elat

Gulf of Aqaba

The Land

Israel's land is in three main strips. Along the Mediterranean Sea lies a large, flat area of land, or **plain**. Toward the middle of Israel is a narrow piece of hills. In the south these hills include the Negev. The Negev is a very dry area that covers about half the country. Inland from the hills is the Jordan River valley.

The Negev is a desert in southern Israel.

The Jordan River flows from north to south. It connects Israel's only two bodies of water. One of these is the Dead Sea, which contains the world's saltiest water. The other body of water is the Sea of Galilee, or Lake Tiberias.

A boat sails on the Sea of Galilee.

7

An oak tree in a nature
reserve in Israel

Plants and Animals

Trees once covered much of Israel.
Most trees were cleared away long
ago for farming, sheepherding, and
cities. But in the last 100 years,
people have planted millions of new
trees in Israel. They include oak,
eucalyptus, and pine. Israel's deserts
are too dry to grow trees well. But
the deserts have a few freshwater
springs. Around these springs grow
lotus trees, reeds, and other plants.

An ibex climbs in the Israeli desert.

Among Israel's wild animals are foxes, hyenas, ibex, wild pigs, and antelopes. Eagles, hawks, and other birds sail through the air. When European storks fly south to Africa for the winter, Israel is on their way. Many storks stop to rest in Israel before continuing on their long journey.

Long Ago

Much of Israel's history is in the Bible. It says that a man named Abraham believed not in many gods but in one God. Abraham's God promised him a new land. He led Abraham to Israel and made him the father of a new people called the **Israelites**. In time, lack of food forced the Israelites into Egypt. They suffered there for many years as slaves. Finally a man named Moses led the Israelites toward Israel. They lived in Israel for many, many years.

In this stone carving, Moses leads the Israelites toward Israel.

The Israelites, or **Jews**, had kings of their own. But soon other groups and kingdoms took over. The Romans were one group that ruled over the Jews for many years. The Romans destroyed the Jews' temple and their capital, Jerusalem. The Jews scattered to other countries. But in the late 1800s, Jews from Russia and other lands started coming back to Israel to live.

The Western Wall in Jerusalem includes part of an ancient Jewish temple.

Israel Today

The Israeli army remembers its fallen soldiers on Memorial Day in 2006.

When the Jews began returning to Israel, it had a different name—Palestine. People called **Arabs** lived there. As Jewish newcomers settled in Palestine, fighting began. The Arabs did not want a Jewish state in Palestine. There was an international plan to split Palestine into two states—one Jewish, the other Arab. The Arabs didn't agree to the plan. But on May 14, 1948, Israel declared itself a homeland for Jewish people.

In the war that followed, Israel gained more land. This made the Palestinian Arabs even more angry. Ever since, there has been a lot of fighting between Israel and the Palestinians. There have also been fights between Israel and its neighbors, including a 2006 conflict with groups in Lebanon.

Did you know?

In western Jerusalem is Yad Vashem. It has museums, exhibits, documents, monuments, sculptures, and memorials to the 6 million Jews killed by **Nazis** during World War II (1939–1945). The ceiling of Yad Vashem's Hall of Names (above) displays photographs of just 600 victims of the **Holocaust**.

An Israeli Arab boy in the city of Acre carries pita bread on his head.

The People

Israel is the only country in the world in which most of the people are Jews. Israel's European Jews are called Ashkenazim. Its Asian and African Jews are called Sephardim. Jews born in Israel are sometimes called Sabra, after a cactus fruit that is prickly on the outside but sweet on the inside. Some say that is how the people are, too!

The rest of Israel's people are mainly Arab. Unlike the Jews, who practice the Jewish faith, most Arabs in Israel are **Muslims**, which means they follow the Islamic religion.

Did you know?

The Hebrew word for "hello" and "good-bye" is the same. It is *shalom*, which means "peace." The Arabic word *salaam* has similar meanings.

14

Israeli children from Russia and Ethiopia have fun in the playground together.

A crowded street in Haifa

City Life and Country Life

An Israeli man works on a kibbutz.

Most Israelis live in cities. The cities are often big, with tall buildings and crowded streets. A city family usually lives in an apartment. Some people live in houses on the edges of cities.

In the country, Israelis may live in a special kind of village called a **kibbutz**. A kibbutz is a farm or settlement in Israel where people work together. Members raise crops for the whole community instead of just themselves. Many of the first kibbutzim in the early 1900s were in dry or dangerous areas. Sharing crops helped feed every kibbutz member. These days some kibbutzim also have companies that develop software for computers!

17

Schools and Language

In Israel, children must go to school until they are 16 years old. There are public schools for Jews and Arabs. In addition to the usual school subjects, Jewish children study the Bible, the Jewish faith, and Jewish culture. Arab children study Muslim faith and culture and the holy book called the Koran.

Hebrew and Arabic are Israel's main languages. Jewish schools use Hebrew, but students may study Arabic, too. Arabic schools use Arabic, but students also study Hebrew starting in the fourth grade. Because people from many different countries

Israeli schoolchildren pose in Tel Aviv by a statue of Israeli prime minister Yitzhak Rabin, who was murdered in 1995.

have moved to Israel, many other languages are spoken, too. Many children learn English in school or at home. Russian has also become a common language in Israel.

A specialist inspects the work of a diamond-polishing machine in Israel.

Work

This tree developed in Israel grows five different kinds of fruit!

Many Israelis are very hardworking. They make computers, books, medical equipment, and medicines. Some Israelis are skilled at cutting diamonds in beautiful ways. In fact, Israel leads the world in diamond cutting and polishing—even though it has no diamonds of its own. Israel must bring diamonds in from other countries.

Israel is a hot, dry land. Even so, Israelis make the most of what they have. They get table salt and other minerals from the Dead Sea. They use the little water they have to grow cotton, barley, wheat, almonds, vegetables, and fruit, especially oranges and grapefruit. More and more, Israelis are using sunshine to make electricity. Plenty of sunshine is one thing Israel has!

Food

Like their Middle Eastern neighbors, Israelis enjoy lamb, rice, eggplant, pita bread, and a smooth sesame-seed paste called tahini. They also eat lots of fresh fruit and vegetables. Israel's European Jews have introduced other food. These foods include chicken soup, chopped liver, a Russian beet soup called borscht, and potato fritters, or latkes. Israel, land of many peoples, also has dishes ranging from Vietnamese egg rolls to American hamburgers.

Plates of olives, dried fruit, pita bread, and hummus (ground chickpeas mixed with tahini)

An Israeli girl prepares dinner for Shabbat, a day of rest and prayer that starts sundown Friday.

Did you know?

The Jewish religion has strict rules about food. Jews may eat only certain animals for food. They may not eat meat and milk products at the same meal. Certain Jews in Israel as well as other places in the world are careful to follow these rules.

Pastimes

Israelis have fun in many of the same ways Americans do. They especially like to read, go to concerts and movies, and watch basketball and soccer on television. At the Dead Sea,

Swimmers float in the Dead Sea.

people love to float on the thick, salty water. It won't let them sink, even if they can't swim.

Israel has a number of large events during the year. One is the annual Jerusalem March, during which thousands of Israelis and people from other countries walk together to the capital city of Jerusalem. Other events include marathons for runners. Every four years Israel holds the Maccabiah Games for Jewish athletes from around the world. Of course, Israeli athletes also compete in the Olympics.

A father and child at the Jerusalem March

25

Holidays

For everyday life, Israelis use the same calendar most Americans do. But for holidays, Jewish Israelis use the Jewish calendar. One Jewish holiday is Passover. During Passover, Jews thank God for bringing them out of Egypt. Israel's Muslims, who are mostly Arabs, have their own calendar, too. They use it for Muslim holidays. One is 'Id al Adha, when Muslims celebrate Abraham's strong faith in God. Israel's Christians celebrate their own holidays, including Christmas and Easter.

Israel is a very important country because two of the world's religions—Christianity and Judaism—started there. Israel is also important to the Muslim religion. Israel is a good place to learn about these three religions. Israel may be a young country, but it has a rich history.

An Israeli family celebrates the Jewish holiday of Passover.

Area: 8,000 square miles (20,770 square kilometers)—slightly smaller than the size of New Jersey

Population: About 6 million people

Capital City: Jerusalem

Other Important Cities: Tel Aviv, Haifa, and Elat

Money: The New Israeli Shekel (NIS)

National Language: Hebrew and Arabic

National Holiday: Independence Day is celebrated in either April or May. While Israel declared independence on May 14, 1948, it falls on the fifth day of the month Iyar according to the Jewish calendar.

Head of Government: The prime minister of Israel

Head of State: The president of Israel

National Flag: A white flag with two blue horizontal stripes, colors found in a Hebrew prayer shawl. Between the stripes is a blue star with six points known as the *Magen David*, or "shield of David."

National Song: "The Hope" (or *"Hatikvah"*). Galician poet Naphtali Herz Imber wrote the words to this song in 1886. Samuel Cohen, an immigrant from Moldavia, arranged the music.

> As long as deep in the heart
> The soul of a Jew is murmuring,
> And to the edges of the East
> And eye towards Zion is watching,
> Still our hope is not lost,
> The hope of two thousand years,
> To be a free people in our land:
> The land of Zion and Jerusalem.

Famous People:

Shmuel Yosef Agnon: cowinner of the Nobel Prize for Literature in 1966

Yael Arad: first Israeli Olympic medalist, in judo

Daniel Barenboim: pianist and conductor

Menachem Begin: prime minister of Israel from 1977 to 1983 and cowinner of the Nobel Peace Prize in 1978

David Ben-Gurion: first prime minister of Israel, from 1948 to 1953, and then 1955 to 1963

Martin Buber: religious philosopher

Golda Meir: prime minister of Israel from 1969 to 1974

Itzhak Perlman: violinist

Anna Ticho: painter

Chaim Topol: film and theater actor

Golda Meir

Israeli Folklore: The Trial of the Egg

Two shepherds eat lunch. The first shepherd, still hungry, asks the second shepherd for his boiled egg and promises to replace it later. The second shepherd never replaces the egg. The first shepherd is angry and demands money from the second shepherd. He says that the egg would have hatched into a hen who in turn would have hatched more eggs. They take the matter to King David, who rules in favor of the angry shepherd. Prince Solomon, then only a child, disagrees with his father's ruling and makes a clever plan that proves the king wrong.

29

How Do You Say...

ENGLISH	HEBREW	HOW TO SAY IT
hello	shalom	sha-LOHM
good-bye	shalom	sha-LOHM
please	b'vakasha	b'VAH-kah-shah
thank you	toda	toh-DAH
one	ahat	ah-HAHT
two	shtayim	sh'TAH-yim
three	shalosh	SHAH-losh
Israel	Israel	YISS-rah-ell

Glossary

Arabs (AH-rabs) Arabs are a group of people who live in the Middle East. Some Arabs live in Israel.

Holocaust (HOL-uh-kost) The Holocaust was the killing of millions of European Jews and others by the Nazis during World War II (1939–1945).

Israelites (IZ-ray-el-ites) The Israelites were the people of the first kingdom of Israel. When food got scarce, the Israelites had to leave Israel and fled to Egypt.

Jews (JOOZ) Jews are people who belong to the Jewish religion. Most of Israel's people are Jews.

kibbutz (kih-BUUTZ) A kibbutz is a farm or settlement where people work together in Israel. On a kibbutz, people share the crops they grow and the things they make.

Muslims (MUHS-lihms) Followers of the Islamic religion are called Muslims. Some Israelis are Muslims.

Nazis (NOT-seez) The Nazis were a political group led by Adolf Hilter that ruled Germany from 1933 to 1945. The Nazis were responsible for killing 6 million Jews during World War II.

plain (PLANE) A plain is a large, flat area of land. Israel has a plain along the Mediterranean Sea.

Further Information

Read It

Bowden, Rob. *Jerusalem*. Milwaukee, WI: World Almanac Library, 2006.

Fontes, Justine and Ron. *Israel*. Danbury, CT: Children's Press, 2003.

Landau, Elaine. *Israel*. Danbury, CT: Children's Press, 2000.

Look It Up

Visit our Web page for lots of links about Israel:
http://www.childsworld.com/links.html

Note to Parents, Teachers, and Librarians: We routinely verify our Web links to make sure they are safe, active sites—so encourage your readers to check them out!

Index

animals, 9
area, 4
Bible, 10, 18
Dead Sea, 7, 21
education, 18–19
farming, 8, 17, 21
food, 10, 21, 22
government, 12
history, 10–11, 12
holidays, 26
industries, 21
Jerusalem, 11, 25
kibbutzim, 17
kingdoms, 21
Koran, 18
languages, 18–19
natural resources, 21
plants, 8, 14
religion, 14, 26
rivers, 6, 7
sports, 24–25